Mason

W9-CBD-098

For Susan Fowler-Gallagher and Robert Hastings,
and the dogs of Black Sheep Farm

ALADDIN PAPERBACKS
An imprint of Simon & Schuster Children's Publishing Division
1230 Avenue of the Americas, New York, NY 10020
Copyright © 2003 by Alice Provensen
All rights reserved, including the right of reproduction in whole or in part in any form.
ALADDIN PAPERBACKS and colophon are trademarks of Simon & Schuster, Inc.
Also available in a Simon & Schuster Books for Young Readers hardcover edition.
Designed by Alice Provensen
The text of this book was set in Futura.
The illustrations for this book were rendered in oils.
Manufactured in China
First Aladdin Paperbacks edition June 2006
10 9 8 7 6 5 4 3 2 1
The Library of Congress has cataloged the hardcover edition as follows:
Provensen, Alice.
A day in the life of Murphy / Alice Provensen.
p. cm.
Summary: Murphy, a farm terrier, describes a day in his life as he gets fed in the kitchen, hunts mice, goes to the vet, returns to the house for dinner, investigates a noise outside, and retires to the barn for sleep.
ISBN-13: 978-0-689-84884-1 (hc.)
ISBN-10: 0-689-84884-6 (hc.)
1. Terriers—Juvenile fiction. [1. Terriers—Fiction. 2. Dogs—Fiction.
3. Farm life—Fiction. 4. Pets—Fiction.] I. Title.
PZ10.3.P928 Day 2003 [E]—dc21 2002004309
ISBN-13: 978-1-4169-1800-4 (Aladdin pbk.)
ISBN-10: 1-4169-1800-0 (Aladdin pbk.)

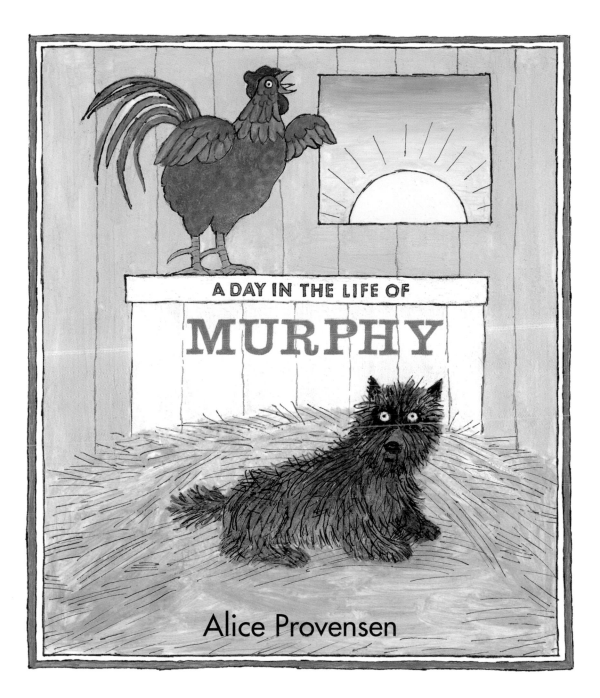

A DAY IN THE LIFE OF

MURPHY

Alice Provensen

ALADDIN PAPERBACKS
New York London Toronto Sydney

MURPHY-STOP-THAT IS MY NAME. I AM A TERRIER. I BARK.
I BARK AT ANYTHING AND EVERYTHING AND ALL THE TIME.
I SLEEP IN A BARN WITH A DUMB CAT AND A DUMB HOUND,
AND A LOT OF OTHER DUMB FARM ANIMALS.

LUCKILY I HAVE A NICE WARM BED IN THE BARN.
THERE IS ONLY ONE TROUBLE WITH SLEEPING THERE.

WHEN WE ALL WAKE UP IN THE MORNING I KNOW I MUST HURRY.

I MUST PAY ATTENTION.

HURRY UP! HURRY UP!   RUN! RUN!   DON'T WASTE ANY TIME.

YOU HAVE TO BE FIRST!   THE FIRST ONE IN THE KITCHEN IN THE MORNING.

WHERE'S THE PAN?   THE PAN FIRST.   LEFTOVERS.   SCRAPS.

THE FLOOR!   THE FLOOR.   NOSE OVER EVERY INCH.

THAT DELICIOUS PILE OF SHOES.   I JUST CAN'T RESIST GIVING THEM A CHEW.

FORGET THE LETTUCE.   WHERE'S THE BOWL?   THE MILK'S SOURING.

CRUMBS.   BITS.   GOOD DROPS OF GREASE.

MURPHY STOP THAT! THEY SAY.   OH-OH, SPANKING.   OUT I GO.

I'M IN AGAIN.
JOHN, THAT BIG OLD
HOUND DOG, GOT IN TOO.

AND THERE'S THAT DUMB CAT NAMED TOM. TOM FOOL, I SAY, BUT
I HAVE TO ADMIT HE HAS CLEVER PAWS. *SCRATCH!* HOOK! HE CAN OPEN
CUPBOARDS. WE ALL KNOW THERE ARE GOOD, CRUNCHY THINGS INSIDE.

I DO ALL THE WORK CHASING TOM AWAY, BUT
I NEVER GET EVEN ONE LITTLE CRACKER. YOU CAN SEE WHY.

THE KITCHEN IS MY FAVORITE PLACE. THERE'S A MOUSE UNDER THE SINK,
SOMEWHERE BEHIND ALL THAT SNEEZY SOAP. I CAN'T SEE HIM; I CAN *SMELL* HIM.
TOO BAD I CAN'T GRAB HIM. OH, WELL. LICK THE LEAKY WATER PIPE.

THERE'S ANOTHER MOUSE UNDER THE STOVE. I KNOW HE'S THERE. JOHN
KNOWS HE'S THERE. WE CAN *SEE* HIM, BUT WE CAN'T GRAB *HIM* EITHER.
OH, WELL. THE STOVE IS MAKING GLORIOUS SOUNDS AND SMELLS.

OH, HOW I LOVE THE STOVE!
MEAT LOAF BAKING.
CHICKEN ROASTING.
PIES SPILLING OVER!

AH, THE GLORY OF IT!
COOKIES!
CAKES!
PUDDINGS!

BANGING PANS! HUMMINGS! COOKINGS AND FRYINGS! BUBBLINGS AND GURGLINGS!

THE JOY!
CREAM! BUTTER!
SALT SHAKINGS!
SUGAR SPRINKLES!

FORGET THE LETTUCE . . .

HONK!
HONK!
HONK!
HONK!

SOMEONE'S HONKING!

IT WAS HONKING FOR ME . . . I SHOULD HAVE GONE INTO HIDING.

LOTS OF DOGS RIDE WITH THEIR HEADS OUT THE WINDOW,
BIG SMILES ON THEIR FACES, TONGUES LOLLING OUT.
EARS FLAPPING IN THE BREEZE . . .

NOT ME! I HATE TO RIDE IN THE CAR.

WHIRRING.
BUMPING.
SWAYING.

WHIMPER.
WHINE.

SICK-MAKING SMELLS OF GAS.

DIZZYING SCENERY.
AIRLESS FOGGING WINDOWS.

HORNS BARKING!
SIRENS SCREAMING!
TIRES SQUEALING!

SNIVEL.
GRUMBLE.
GROAN.
ARE WE THERE YET?

D.V.M.

I KNOW WHERE I AM. I'VE BEEN HERE BEFORE.

THERE'S A ROOM WHERE SAD, NERVOUS DOGS AND WHIMPERING PUPPIES ARE WAITING.

ALL WAITING.   WAITING.   WAITING.   WAITING FOR THE VET.

I THINK I MAY HAVE TO THROW UP.

OH-OH, IT'S MY TURN TO BE . . .

PINCHED . . . POKED . . . PRODDED. DOESN'T HURT, BUT GET ME OUT OF HERE!

HOME!

HEAD FOR THE HOUSE!

HURRY UP! HURRY UP!

DON'T WASTE ANY TIME!

DINNER MUST BE READY!

HIDE IN THE FOREST OF KITCHEN CHAIR LEGS BENEATH THE OILCLOTH LEAVES.
SSSH-H-H. BE QUIET . . . BE PATIENT. DON'T BEG.

THINGS DROP.   CRUMBS.   GOOD THINGS.   SNEAKY HANDOUTS.
KEEP AN EYE ON THE DOG DISH.   THERE MIGHT BE LEFTOVERS!

WHERE IS EVERYONE? IT'S BEDTIME.
THEY'VE PROBABLY ALL GONE TO BED.

IT'S DARK OUT. I'M TIRED.
I SHOULD BE IN BED TOO.

WAIT! WHAT WAS THAT?
WHO'S OUT THERE?

WHAT WAS THAT SOUND?
SOMETHING'S HAPPENING!

MURPHY!
GET A HOLD OF YOURSELF!

YOU'LL MAKE
EVERYONE ANGRY.

BARK!
BARK!

BARK
BARK

BARK
BARK
BARK

BARK
BARK!

BARK!
BARK!

BARK

BARK!

BARK

WAS IT A RAT?   A FOX?   A SKUNK?   A WOLF?   A BEAR?   A THIEF?

THE MOON!   THE MOON!   I HEARD THE MOON MOVE!

THE BARN'S NOT A BAD PLACE AFTER ALL. IT'S WARM AND FRIENDLY
AND THERE'S LOTS OF HAY TO CURL UP IN. SMELLS GOOD TOO.

DEAR SOCK. GOOD OLD BONE. GOOD OLD STICK. SIGH.
GOOD NIGHT.